A Coffee Date

Debanjali Mukherjee

BLUEROSE PUBLISHERS
India | U.K.

Copyright © Debanjali Mukherjee 2023

All rights reserved by author. No part of this publication may be reproduced, stored in a retrieval system or transmitted in any form or by any means, electronic, mechanical, photocopying, recording or otherwise, without the prior permission of the author. Although every precaution has been taken to verify the accuracy of the information contained herein, the publisher assume no responsibility for any errors or omissions. No liability is assumed for damages that may result from the use of information contained within.

BlueRose Publishers takes no responsibility for any damages, losses, or liabilities that may arise from the use or misuse of the information, products, or services provided in this publication.

For permissions requests or inquiries regarding this publication, please contact:

BLUEROSE PUBLISHERS
www.BlueRoseONE.com
info@bluerosepublishers.com
+91 8882 898 898
+4407342408967

ISBN: 978-93-5819-379-4

First Edition: September 2023

I dedicate my first attempt at seeing myself as a writer to my inspiration without whom I would never have reinvented myself. Kudos to your extraordinary insight. You have restored the lost faith in myself, You have given me the strength to fly with wings of desire.

And special thanks to my life partner who has never left any of my wishes unfulfilled

About the Story

Life is an ongoing process. Sometimes life goes on in its own peaceful course, sometimes a storm comes and destroys everything. Rishav and Jiya fall in love with each other and begin their journey of life, then marriage, and then comes the storm. The storm was predicted in advance, but it was too late to realize it. Days change, but true love never changes. However, even if love is true, can all love be reconciled? When a loved one suddenly disappears, the whole world turns dark in an instant. Coming from dark to light is a beautiful thing, but going back from light to dark makes darkness seem even denser. Is it possible to bring back the light by fighting with that thick darkness? Will Rishav be able to bring back the light of his life, his Jiya, or will he himself be lost in that darkness? Where will this love story of Rishav and Jiya lead them to the end?

1

"Hi! A beautiful morning is waiting for you to wake up. Go to your balcony, see the sun shining for you, the birds chirping for you, and the beautiful flowers in the garden blooming just for you."

It's so nice to hear the notification tone on the phone at exactly 6 am these days. I feel like I can go to sleep peacefully at night just because I can hear this sweet melody in the morning. Now I can work all day feeling less tired. The sun seems a little brighter these days, the front garden looks more beautiful than I've ever felt before, I feel a lot more confident now, I feel like I can tackle all odds without hesitation.

This morning melody fills my whole day with a beautiful rhythm. And now I replied, "A very good morning to you."

Morning is the busiest time of the day.
1.5 hours seem to pass in just 1.5 minutes. Sent 2-3 more messages while preparing breakfast. Then, after getting ready, I dropped Ron off at his school. At exactly 8 o'clock I entered my office. It was a very hectic day. Besides taking classes, I had to attend a meeting. It was 4 pm, and I left my office. Probably Ron is playing with his granny now. I was just thinking about Ron.

As soon as I started the car, I got a message on my phone, "Today I feel like grabbing a coffee."
Oh, it's him.
I replied, smiling, "Well, have it. What's the problem?"
The answer came from the other side, "Together."
Again I smiled and replied, "How is that possible? You are far away in another country."
"No ma'am, now in your city," came the reply.
"O, really! What a pleasant surprise.", I replied.
Then again his message came, "So, would you allow me to take just one hour out of your busy schedule as I know you spend this time with your son everyday."
"It would be great if I could honor your invitation. But I'm really very sorry as I have to take my mother to the doctor this evening" was my reply.
Again the message tone beeped, "No problem. Can we make it tomorrow evening?"

Perhaps it is called a hell-bent person, not ready to give up in any way. However, somehow I started loving this man's stubborn attitude.

"Sure, why not" I sent the reply and started driving home.

A busy day followed by a busy evening. How fast the clock struck 9 tonight. After finishing our dinner, I went to bed early.

I sent the message "Good Night" and placed the phone on the side table.

As I laid my head on the pillow, many conflicting questions came to my mind before I fell asleep. Who is this man? Why do I like to talk to him so much? I haven't even met this guy. But his words are very touching. Talking to him makes me smile from the heart, and I feel pain inside at the same time. Why, why, why? Why do his words touch me so deeply? Why very few people can touch our hearts despite being so far away. How just one message from this guy can make my day so much better than thousands of people around me can't.

Just over six months ago I started a conversation with that guy on a social dating site. When I left my country 2 years ago after losing everything and came here, I decided that I will never tie myself to any other relationship in life. I had deleted all my accounts from social media more than three years ago. I don't talk too much except talking to people related to my work. I return home from work, don't go anywhere else unless I have to. Sometimes I only meet with my classmate Arushi.

Arushi, my dear friend, without whom I could not start all over again. Who suddenly came and saved my life like an angel about two years eight months ago. I was frantically looking for a job at that time. My son Ron was very young, only four months old. I was proletarian then. My father passed away shortly after I left everything and moved to my paternal home. After my father's death I left our rented apartment in Delhi and moved to our own house in Chandigarh with my mother. We were somehow living on the money my father had saved throughout his life. I was pregnant then, my mother was handling everything alone. We moved to Chandigarh and exactly three months later my son Ronit was born. Ronit, my son, was my means of survival then, and my mother. They had given me the strength to fight that time. But it was becoming difficult to run the family from the accumulated money. My son was very young. The cost of our living was going up a lot day by day. Amidst this turmoil, I suddenly met Arushi one day. Leaving my son at home with my mother I went to a job interview. I was sitting at a coffee shop out there. Alone. Tired. Destitute. Just then someone said "Hey Jiya" standing next to me. Just seeing I hugged Arushi. I brought her to our house. I attended her wedding two years ago. After marriage she moved to New Jersey. Her husband settled there. They came here on vacation. Arushi's in-law's house is in Chandigarh. I Met her after a long time. That day we had a long conversation and we shared a lot with each other. Then she came to know everything and scolded me for blindly trusting our friend, the impostor. After that, I can never repay what my dearest friend did for me. Her husband helped me to get a job in

New Jersey. Leaving everything in India, I moved to New Jersey with my mother and my little son to live anew. My son just turned 1 year old then.

In a new country, in an unknown city, my new struggle to survive began. My mother and my little son, they are my whole world now. It is because of them that I am still alive. After dinner they go to bed early, then I spend some alone time with myself.

Suddenly one evening, I got very bored and randomly created that account on a social dating site with a fake name and talked to some people which annoyed me even more. So I put aside the thought and took a long walk that evening. Alone. As soon as I got home I jumped into my bed and fell asleep in no time.

After exactly one month I was busy working in the office and suddenly a message came on that dating site, it said "Hi". Just a "Hi", nothing more. I didn't care to answer and forgot later. The next evening, I received another message, "A beautiful woman never forgets to answer, even to the most annoying person in the world." Suddenly, I angrily replied, "So, now you have understood that I am the ugliest woman."
The reply came, "Wow! That's a very nice answer. I'm sure, you are beautiful."
"No", I immediately stopped replying.

The next day I was checking my phone. The man sent another message last night, "How did you know that? Someone who can give such a nice answer must be very beautiful."

"Okay. Be very happy thinking that," I replied.

Immediately I got the answer, "Although you are beautiful, but your typing speed is very slow, it took you so long to write just this one line! Okay. No problem. You will learn to type faster after a few days if you chat with me continuously."

"Haha. Very funny" I replied.

"That means you're smiling now. Thank God I managed to make you smile a little", I got the reply.

I don't know why suddenly I cried at this. I immediately went to the washroom. After that I did not give any answer. There was no message from him that day either.

Another message came the next evening, "At least you can invite me to your house for tea because I made you smile."

"Okay, please come to my house. My mom will make tea for you. I can't do it now, because I'm going to my work", I replied.

"Are you going to work now? Do you work the night shift?" He asked.

"No. I am a school teacher", I replied.

"Oh. Which country are you living in?" He immediately asked.

Oh god. That means he wants to know my whereabouts, my details.

"Utopia", I replied immediately.

Reply came, "Very funny"

"So you owe a tea invitation to me now", I answered.

"Oh, please come," he replied again.

"Well, tell me, if you lend me some money, and after a few days I lend you the same amount of money, how much money will we pay back to whom in the end?" I replied.

"Nothing", he replied.

"Yes. So this time I'm not going to your house", was my immediate answer.

"How easily you figured out the calculation. Are you a math teacher?, he asked again.

"Unfortunately yes", I replied.

"Why is that unfortunate?", he asked again.

"Because, I couldn't ever solve the mathematical calculations of my life", I wrote immediately.

Thus we started talking to each other..

And we continued to chat….

After that we shared a lot, but I never asked him about his personal life. Once he told me that he lives alone in his apartment in Bangalore, not his own, but given to him by the office. He didn't ask me anything about my personal life, except one thing, who I am living with now. I told him with my mother and my only son. After that we never inquired about anything personal.

It continued like this, sometimes talking in messages, nothing more than that. The guy is very funny, but while talking, it seems that there is buried sadness somewhere inside him. But I never asked him about it and neither did he. In my life there is also the pain of losing everything. So we never discussed these things.

A lot of work has to be done at home during the weekends. I will leave at 5 pm today. A coffee date. With the guy I don't know.

2

When I was a teenager, I had very bad habits. I used to talk too much. At that time, one day we three friends were studying at a friend Sunil's house. Five boys were hanging out in the yard of the front house, playing loud music. Sunil showed one of them and said, "This is the guy's house, his name is Rishav. The rest of the boys are his friends. Tomorrow is the wedding of that Rishav's sister. That's probably why they are playing loud music."

After a few days I went to that friend Sunil's house again. And the guy, Rishav from that front house came there for some reason. Seeing him, I yelled very loudly, "How are you? You live in the front house, don't you?"
He answered me very calmly, "I'm fine. You?"
This time again I shouted, "I'm well too."
Now he asked me calmly, "Well, did you accidentally eat a microphone at breakfast today?"
With all my might, I replied, "No. Why?"
Rishav asked again, "So are you always so loud?"
I replied, "No. I thought you might have trouble hearing the low voice."
"Why do you think so?" he asked in surprise.
"You were listening to music so loud that day," I pretended to be surprised. He just laughed.

This is how we started talking at my friend's house. After a few days we gave each other our contact number. We became good companions. Though he was four years older than me, age couldn't ruin our beautiful friendship. After dating for a few years we decided to get married. I got a job at a college. Rishav got the job before me, but we waited. We got married only after I joined the service. I remember a little incident from our wedding day. Rishav and I were talking a lot on the phone on that day. Rishav even called me on the way to my home. Then one of Rishav's friends jokingly said, "If you say everything now, what will you do after marriage?" Then the rest of his friends laughed and said, "Now let them say whatever they want. There is so much to do after marriage, why waste time just talking then?" After hearing this I immediately hung up the phone. All the wedding rituals were done very nicely. After everything was completed I went to their house with Rishav.

The days were going very well, just like a dream. I didn't know how to do any household work. I never played any role other than a student in my life before marriage. Since then, a little problem started in my in-law's house. At first, my parents-in-law objected to marrying their son with a working lady. Later they requested me to quit the job after my marriage. And I couldn't keep that request. They were saddened by this. I used to study at home after taking classes in college. Since then problems started with me at home. My in-laws requested my husband to convince me that my family should also be given importance. I should learn housework so that they can have free time and go to visit different places now. So I thought of quitting my job and starting my own business. I thought I could devote time to my own business as I liked, and I could spend more time at home.

So I started my own business with all the money I saved from my job. But that was not enough. Then Rishav put all his money into my business. Business continued and started growing. Then I was giving more time to my business. I could not spend much time at home anymore. I felt so guilty. I moved to business thinking that I could spend more time at home, but I was doing the exact opposite. My parents-in-law rarely spoke to me. They were not happy with my behavior. Again, I felt helpless. My husband has stopped showing any interest in my business as well as personal matters. He told me, "Moving to business was entirely your decision. You know very well how to manage everything."

This was the first time when my husband was not ready to support my work. But he never asked me to give up on my dream of becoming a successful woman. I could sense that he was feeling indecisive about who to support, his parents or his wife. My romantic, vivacious, chatty husband was gradually becoming very silent these days.

It was a very difficult time for both of us. One day I was late to return home. Had some client meetings. It was my parents-in-law's wedding anniversary. I was told to come home early that day. I could not leave this important responsibility to others and return home early. When I returned home, no one spoke to me that night. I was a little afraid and sad. Couldn't manage to get home early the next few days, as my business was booming and I needed to invest more time there. And right then my husband suddenly decided that both of us will leave my in-laws house and live separately so that I don't have to face any problem to work. Oh god, my husband still loves my craziness as much as ever. How lucky I am! Immediately I wanted to hold him tightly in my arms. That night was so beautiful, unlike other nights, neither of us could sleep. Caught in each other's arms, we spent planning where we would stay, what we would do there, how to decorate our new home, and everything. Hand in hand we were feeling each other's words very closely. The next few days were very busy. Finding a new house, decorating it, then packing all our belongings and moving in. Rishav found this house. Double storey building. The house is surrounded by a boundary wall, with an iron gate in front. The front side of the ground floor is mostly empty for parking. There is a large room at the rear of the ground floor. The electrical room was also on the ground floor, and there was a water pump room. The stairs leading to the second floor pass by it. After going up to the second floor, opening the door, first there was a living room. Adjacent to the living room was a large balcony. On one side of the living room was the kitchen and next to it was the bathroom attached to a bedroom. And on the other side there were two more bedrooms and a bathroom. The house is big for two people, but very nice. The house was about twenty years old, but looked very nice after renovation. I liked the house very much.

First conversation with my husband, then friendship, then love and marriage, and then starting our life anew in our new home, a few years passed in between.

Just a few days before my marriage, my friend Sunil, who lived just behind my in-law's house, suddenly moved to their village with his family. His father had a business, the business was running at such a loss that his father went bankrupt at that time. But after being neighbors for a long time they became very close friends of my in-laws. Even after moving to the village permanently, my friend used to visit my in-laws' house occasionally. I could not meet my friend all the time because I did not stay at home every time. I used to remain busy with my office and business. Time just flew by. A few days before moving into our new apartment, my parents-in-law made a request to me. They told me, "You can't do any household work properly by yourself, how will you manage business and family simultaneously after moving there? You can do one thing. You can take your friend Sunil to your business. It will help you a lot in your work. But this is just a suggestion. You can also reject it if you want. You have never accepted any of our requests. If you don't listen today, we won't get any new sorrow."

Their words suddenly hit me like a whip. I could sense that they were very hurt by our decision to separate from them. My husband and I said together, "Your advice is like a blessing to us." But I could not understand why my husband was not very happy with the decision to involve my friend in my business. But did not say anything as this was his parents' decision. Later my sister-in-law Rohini also said that it was not a very good decision to associate Sunil with my business. But I could not hurt my parents-in-law by removing Sunil from there.

Since then the time has been very difficult. I could not do the housework properly despite my best efforts. I used to mess something up every day. And I could learn many new things from these mistakes every day. My husband used to help me in all my work. Though we both made many mistakes every day, these mistakes made together were a new joy for us every day. During the day we were busy with our own work outside the house. We used to come back home at night very tired and could not eat properly. We didn't have time or energy to cook properly. Our house was messy. Then we hired a maid to work in our house for the whole day. As a result, none of us would return home early. We gave more attention to our work. We used to return home late at night after finishing work. Then we went to sleep very tired. The conversation between me and my husband decreased a lot that time.

My friend Sunil helped me a lot in my business. Even then I could not return home quickly. An unknown distance started forming between me and my husband. None of us understood that at first. My husband used to come home before me most days. He used to wait for me. When I came home we would eat together and go to sleep. And for my business, I started getting late back home. Despite many efforts, I could not return home early. Then my husband came home and fell asleep waiting for me without having dinner.

After I returned home, Rishav did not wake up to have dinner. Both of us would then go to sleep without having dinner. But this way can not continue for long. I requested Rishav to take dinner instead of waiting for me. This is how we were slowly losing the beautiful moments we used to spend together at dinner. Our old beautiful times, familiar moments kept changing. And like all familiar things, we also kept changing. Even though we were in the same house as husband and wife, the distance between us continued to grow. Now none of us seem to know each other. We could not understand each other's words and feelings properly. Neither of us realized that even though we lived so close, we were drifting apart. We kept thinking that money will buy us happiness, so we rushed to make more money without giving each other time. We went to buy happiness with money, and instead, we got more and more emotional distance between us.

My oldest and best friend is now my secretary in my business. I was lucky to have such a friend, who helped me a lot in business. Every day he was looking for new clients. I had to go with him sometimes. Then we used to have meetings in the office for a long time. Sunil used to insist me not to go home until the whole job was done. But I used to return home leaving work incomplete sometimes, because my husband was waiting for me at home. Even when I came back home, Sunil sat in the office and finished all the work and then went home. And he completed the work accurately. After that, I didn't have much to do, except to carefully look over the files and sign those. He was doing his job very sincerely. Sunil and I were working together and my business was improving a lot, but I could spend less time at home. I was getting very depressed. Sunil noticed that. He told me that now he can do everything accurately, so I should spend more time at home. What is a good friend if not like this... Not everyone can understand the mind. After that I gave more responsibility to him. I got a little more free time for myself, and my friend continued to do all the work of my business with more of his time.

But it was too late. We had already created an invisible wall between us. In between I noticed that Rishav remained a bit annoyed at times. For no reason. I don't know why he didn't want to come closer to me anymore. Our warm embrace had grown cold. I banged my head against that invisible wall, trying in vain to break through. I used to smile, hiding an unbearable pain in my heart. As I was breaking from the inside, I was trying to be stronger from the outside. From then on, more and more silent distance began to form between me and my husband. We started arguing about small things. We did not realize that the small cracks in the relationship house will one day cause the whole house to break down. At that time, instead of repairing those cracks, we allowed the cracks to grow. None of us were happy.

I was gloomy in those days. My friend Sunil became my savior again in those days of my depression. He listened to me very carefully and said, "Why are you worrying so much when you have a friend?"
I said to myself, "Thank you God, for giving me such a good friend."

Since then I had become more and more dependent on my friend for business. He handled all the responsibilities more. After that I had more free time to spend with my husband. I didn't have to look at the business side. I had this confidence that I had a friend who would take care of everything. Soon our wedding anniversary was around the corner. "Does Rishav still remember this day?" I was very excited thinking about it. One day my client meeting was going on at the office, and just then my husband's message came, "We are going to Goa for five days to celebrate our anniversary, are you ready to go? Then pack your bags." I could not focus on the meeting. I immediately wanted to go out and dance for joy. Only two days are left to start the journey. Everything must be arranged in it. But my business work and meetings? It would continue for the whole week. Who will handle them if not me? But the time we were going through, we both needed this special moment. The next five days spent together would give our relationship a new lease of life. What should I do, which aspect should I save, my married life or my business? I fell into a dilemma. This time my friend Sunil became my savior once again. He smiled and said to me, "Why do you worry so much? I am still here."

Oh God! Thank you. No more worries. I told Sunil to prepare all papers for the upcoming meetings as soon as possible. I would sign them so that Sunil could continue the meetings in my absence. Only two days left. Everything should be ready in between. I could no longer control myself. I immediately wanted to rush to Goa with Rishav. Couldn't wait for the flight two days later. Time was not moving fast enough to match my excitement. But there was nothing to do. I have to look at my business side as well. Sunil started preparing all the papers very quickly. I would have to check before signing. Sunil is very dedicated in all these work related matters. He just took one day to prepare it. Sunil put a pile of papers in the files on my table the next morning. After an hour there were two important client meetings in a row. I had to finish those two meetings before leaving. Sunil organized those two meetings. I would have to introduce Sunil as my representative to them, so that when I won't be there, my friend could have the next meeting with them.

A lot of work that day. Meeting, then checking all the papers, signing those, then going home and packing. I could not handle anything properly due to excitement. I could not concentrate on anything. The clock seemed to be moving very slowly that day. Somehow I finished all the work and returned home. The next morning flight is at 10 am. When Rishav finished all his work and returned home that night, I was busy packing for our trip. I noticed that Rishav was as excited as me. After finishing all the work when we were going to bed, the phone rang. It's Sunil. Why is Sunil calling now?
"Hello"
"Hello, my dear friend, I know how happy you are tonight. It may not be right to call you at this time. But I was forced to do it", Sunil replied.

"What happened?" I asked him.
What Sunil said, I did not sign all the papers in a hurry. It would be difficult for Sunil to do his work in my absence. But what could be done then? Sunil found another way again. The next day he would come to the airport and get my signature. So I should forget everything and go to sleep peacefully that night.

The next day we reached the airport early. But Sunil was not seen anywhere. Called and found out that his car broke down on the road, so it was a little late. Rishav and I were getting very restless. It was almost time for the flight to take off. There's not much time left. Finally Sunil came. I somehow signed the papers, there was no time to check. Though Sunil repeatedly said to take a look before signing. But where is the time? Signed somehow I quickly entered the airport. Rishav had already entered. He was waiting for me inside.

We reached Goa just in time. Coming here I started to feel how long we have been waiting for this beautiful moment. I was feeling so good that I didn't want to think about anything else. We quickly ate something and went to the beach. We both walked in silence for a long time. It was as if we were feeling each other not with words but with touch. Going a little further, that touch became more emotional. It seemed like we were being swept away by the crazy sea breeze. A lot of time passed in this way. A great wave of love was flowing between us that night. I was slowly melting into Rishav's warmth. We got lost in each other's arms during that beautiful time. How nice it would be if time were stuck there. But no. Those five days passed by. Too soon. I was very upset on the day of our return. I felt like holding time and Rishav together, forever, right there. But had to come back. Back in our hometown. Then the old routine, work, busy life started again.

Sunil had done everything properly. I didn't have to see anything after coming back. The meetings went well. We were going to start working jointly with a new company. I needed to see those papers. I asked Sunil to give me that file, He reminded me that he was going to the lawyer to finish some legal work on the file. He would come back from there and discuss some points with me, it was very important. Yeah, right. First, the legal work should be completed quickly. Fortunately, Sunil takes care of everything. I told him to finish all the work quickly and come back to the office. I kept waiting for him and doing the rest of the work. Sunil was late to finish the work that day. I became impatient and called him again and again. He smiled and said, "Everything will be fine. Now there is no problem, everything is going right, it's just taking a little time."

It was getting late. In the evening, he suddenly called to tell me that everything went well, but there was another problem. Hearing his voice, I felt very worried. Fear and anxiety in his voice. What he said was that, his mother had called, suddenly his father was feeling very ill in the village, and he had to go immediately. He could not understand what to do then. The railway station is very close to where he went. So I had to tell him to go to his village immediately. How could I ask him to come to the office before going? And I didn't have sufficient time to go there to bring that file. Sunil would miss the train.

From there Sunil went to his village and did not come to the office that day. Before leaving, he said he would return one week later. We were going to start working with the new company within the next couple of months. Before that we have to prepare many things ourselves. Sunil went to the village and informed that his father's health had further deteriorated. I started to worry a lot. What would happen now? I didn't see anything, Sunil was taking care of everything. The file also remained with him. But Sunil could not return after one week, he was taking more time because in that situation his mother was not able to handle everything alone.

Meanwhile, I didn't know why, since the last few days, Rishav was looking very upset. I couldn't figure out how to handle that situation. This tension of business, and at home Rishav stopped talking to me. What happened to him, I could not understand anything. No, it couldn't go on like this. I would have to talk to Rishav. I came back home early that day and was waiting for Rishav's return.

I called him again and again. He didn't pick up my phone. I became very worried. Late at night, I suddenly woke up to the notification tone of the phone. Rishav sent a message that he won't return home that night. Rishav had never done this before. What happened to him suddenly? While waiting for Rishav, I fell asleep sitting on the couch in the living room. After seeing Rishav's message, I went to the bedroom. Changed and laid on the bed but could not sleep for the whole night. Didn't know when Rishav would return home. Then I would have to go to the office. I didn't even know if Sunil would come to the office the next day. Sunil also did not send any message. I was very confused about everything. I couldn't understand what was going on in my life. For now, the worry about Rishav started to increase. Rishav returned home in the morning. But why was Rishav looking like this? It seemed as if a storm had passed over him. After returning home, he entered the bedroom and closed the door immediately. I kept knocking from outside the bedroom. He replied to me, "You go to the other bedroom, you don't need to come here." Oh God, what are these Rishav saying! I again waited in the living room for Rishav to open the door. A little later Rishav opened the bedroom door for water. Then I hugged Rishav and kept asking what happened to him, why is he doing this to me, why is he not talking to me. Without giving any answer he opened his laptop bag and continued to take out something from there. Which he took out of the bag and placed in front of me, seeing that I started feeling dizzy. It felt like the ground had moved from under my feet. I didn't remember what happened after that. After a while when I opened my eyes, I saw mom sitting next to me, Rishav went to the other bedroom and closed the door. I started crying. I didn't know how it happened. After a few hours I packed all my stuff and came to my paternal house with my mother. That news which I was waiting to tell Rishav remained untold. Rishav did not open the door of that room when I was leaving. I had to bid him goodbye from outside the closed door. I returned home with a broken heart.

3

I still remember my school days. I had always been very good at studies. At the same time I was very fond of playing football. I wanted to choose football as a career. But there was a lot of objection to it from my house. Four of my school friends, Gaurav, Ravi, Anurag and Nitin were very supportive of my football game. These five of us friends always did everything together. I used to share all my thoughts with them. Many times I used to go to play football matches without informing home. They used to help me with class notes. But many times it was reported from school to home that I was absent. My parents were very angry, but my elder sister supported me. When I left home to study engineering, I used to go straight to the football ground after classes. I became tired and fell asleep after returning to the hostel. Sometimes chatting with friends would go on all night. In the beginning I hardly studied. I was the hero of the football ground. When everyone was there cheering me on, I forgot about the whole world except football. The girls of a college next to that football ground also used to come there to watch my game. It was going well. Here is no one to stop me from playing. But apart from this, I was not doing anything. None of my other four close friends came here to study engineering with me. So I was having a lot of trouble. I had many friends in the hostel and class, but they were not that close to me. In the first year of engineering, the result was very bad. I decided not to go home on vacation after the first year exams. I thought I would play a lot of football for those few days, there is no pressure of studying. But meanwhile, my sister Rohini's marriage was fixed. had to go. At home, my sister was the only supporter of my game, she was my best friend. She would get married, she would leave the house, I was very upset thinking about this. I packed some of my stuff and went home. Before going home, I informed my four friends about my arrival. As soon as I got off the train I saw Ravi, Gaurav, Nitin and Anurag waiting for me at the station. That's what close friends are.

I did not meet my sister after returning home. I was very angry with my sister. Why did she need to get married so soon? If she leaves, I would be alone at home. My parents didn't understand me as much as my elder sister did. Probably I was thinking like a selfish person. But I was really very sad. My sister understood exactly what I was thinking. I came home and sat quietly in the living room, she came, sat by my side and started stroking my head. I don't know what happened to me suddenly, I burst into tears, forgetting all my anger I hugged my elder sister. My elder sister Rohini smiled a little and said, "Don't be upset. I will come here to meet you. When you come from the hostel, inform me in advance. One more thing, keep studying, but don't stop playing." I told her, "Why do you need to get married so soon?" She said, "You know, I was under pressure from

home for a long time to get married, our parents don't even want me to do this job. I have spoken to Manish, my fiancé. He has no objection to my employment."
"I miss you all the time, I will do more after your marriage" I said in reply.
My sister Rohini said, "You freshen up now. We will have lunch together today. I don't know when we will get a chance to eat together again after my marriage. Don't waste your time sitting like this."

Sister's wedding day was almost there. The next day. Instead of being happy at my sister's wedding, I was sad. I called my four friends home. But I didn't want to talk to anyone that day. So we were sitting in the yard listening to music together. The house behind us belongs to Suni's family. My parents had a very good relationship with them. Don't know why, but my sister Rohini never liked Sunil. On the eve of my sister's wedding, I saw two of his friends come to Sunil's house while we were listening to music sitting in the yard. Both are girls. Suddenly it seemed they were talking to each other about us. I didn't like anything else then. But seeing a girl among them from a distance made me feel good. I liked her eyes and her smile.

Rohini's wedding ceremony took place the next day. I was feeling very lonely at home. I decided to return to the hostel before the end of the holiday. Parents were upset at home. My sister had left home, went to her in-laws' house. I would also go back to the hostel after two days.

One day before returning to my hostel, I suddenly had to go to Sunil's house. My mother forced me to go there. Had to go to return some items borrowed from them during Rohini's marriage. I saw that the girl came to their house again. I saw her very closely that day. I felt like staring at her eyes the whole day. But it seemed that the girl was a little annoyed to see me. Yes, that's right. Seeing me, the girl screamed at me, "How are you? You live in the front house, don't you?" I started thinking, "What is this? Is the girl crazy? Or something else. Why is she talking so loudly?" Not understanding anything, I stupidly replied "I'm fine. You?" After talking to her, I realized that she was angry with me for playing music so loudly on the eve of Rohini's wedding. But the girl's anger made me laugh a lot, seeing the way she talked. I thought to myself, let's be friends with this girl. But meanwhile I already said at home that I want to go back to the hostel before the holiday is over. No, the decision had to be changed. This girl is quite interesting. After returning home I informed my parents that I would return to the hostel after a few more days. After my sister's marriage, my parents became sad. They were very happy to hear that I would spend some more time with them.

After that I asked Sunil about that girl. Sunil said that two friends came to his house that day, one was Jiya, and the other was Arushi.

"Oh! I forgot to ask the girl's name that day. So what will happen now?" I thought to myself and I did not ask Sunil anything more after that. But then an opportunity came after days to talk to that girl. After coming home, I was learning to drive a car. Every evening I used to take the car with my father. I noticed that the girl sometimes came out with her bicycle at that time. One day while driving, I saw a crowd of people in front. I told my dad to wait in the car and I went to see what happened. I saw that the girl had fallen from her bicycle and was badly injured. Everyone was trying to lift her from the ground. I brought the girl in our car and took her to a clinic. Then my father and I brought her home. This is how my friendship with her started. The girl's name is Jiya. She was only fifteen then. Their home is in Chandigarh. Came to Delhi only a few months ago. Her father got posted here, so. Sunil and Arushi were her classmates. Apart from Sunil, sometimes Jiya went to Arushi's house.

Since that day, Jiya did not get angry when she saw me. Instead, she smiled sweetly, sometimes she spoke to me. Before I went back to the hostel we took each other's contact numbers. Who knows what happened to me after that. I played football less and focused more on studies. I thought it would take a long time to stabilize my career playing football. I don't have that much time. Soon I would have to be self-sufficient. I used to come home when I got leave. The purpose was to meet Jiya. Just talking on the phone was not enough. I used to share all my thoughts with her. One day I told her about my love for football. Then assured her that I had been paying more attention to my studies than playing football. Hearing this, Jiya was surprised and said, "Why did you divert your focus from that which is your passion?" Hearing this, I thought to myself, "What the hell! Is Jiya not thinking about her future with me?" But after what She said, my respect for her increased a lot. "You should do the work that you like to do from your heart. Otherwise, you will not get job satisfaction by doing your work, you will lose enthusiasm for work very easily. Even if you get less income from the work that you love to do, you will be happy. If you don't find happiness in your work, how will you continue your job in the long run?" If only my parents understood this. But I felt that there is someone in this world who understands me except my sister, Rohini. Only this girl could be my real life partner. After that I continued to enjoy both my studies and playing football equally. Then some beautiful time passed.

I have always been good at studies. So it was not too late for me to get a good job after completion of my studies. Jiya was a college student then. We used to meet on weekends due to my work pressure during weekdays. When I remained very busy at the office, I could not attend calls from my home sometimes. I called them back later. One day Jiya's call came. Twice. Could not receive as usual. We were supposed to meet that evening. I thought I would call her later. Just then, Jiya's message came, Her father suddenly started feeling chest pain, she and her mother were waiting for an ambulance to come. But they were worried because the ambulance was too late. I immediately informed my office, applied for half day leave and went out taking my car. When I reached Jiya's house, the ambulance had not arrived then too. I was waiting for them after taking them to the hospital. Her father had to be admitted to the hospital. After dropping Jiya and her mother at their house, I returned home quite late that night. In the meantime several calls came from my home, as I was getting late to return. I was at the hospital, the phone was silent. And also couldn't talk from there. My parents were very anxious. I could feel their worries. After hearing everything, they were very upset, but did not say anything. After a week her father recovered and returned home. Jiya was very happy that day. That day Jiya cooked something at home. Her mother invited me to dinner. Although the girl had not learnt to cook yet, she tried very hard to cook well.

After a few days, I asked Jiya what she thought about marriage. Hearing this, the crazy girl asked me what I thought about my football career.

I replied, "I have no further plans for that."

And she replied to me, "I have no plans of marriage either."

I wondered, "Why? Don't you like me anymore?"

Jiya was even more surprised and replied, "Don't you like playing football anymore?" Jiya also said, "If you can let go of your first love, I will also learn to let go of my first love."

Phew, this girl can get angry at me for no reason. However, I was very happy to hear that I was her 'first love'.

Now I also showed a little fake anger and said, "I did all this to get you soon. If you don't want me, then it's ok. You are always angry with me and talk sweetly to everyone else. You do not be angry with anyone like this. If you don't marry me, who will you be angry with for the rest of your life?"

Jiya smiled and said, "Why, if I don't marry you, you won't allow me to show anger on you?"

I said, "Absolutely not. You will no longer have this right."

Jiya said, "Then what else can be done? Now I have no choice but to marry you."

Then Jiya told me about her wish. Jiya wanted to do something after finishing her studies, a job or her own business. Then she would marry me. She asked me if I could wait for her for that long. I had no problem waiting. But I was a little afraid when I heard that she wanted to do a job or business. Because, this would definitely be objected to from my house. I could not speak more that day. I returned home early saying I would have to do a job.

"There was an objection from home about my sister's job. Will Jiya be accepted from my home?" I was thinking about this after returning home, I have to talk to my sister about this. The next day I spoke to my sister Rohini.
After hearing everything, Rohini said, "Why would a bright student just sit at home after studying so much? I also work. My in-laws don't mind. Jiya will either work or start her own business. You and I will talk to our parents about this together. You don't think so much about these things at all."

Truly, what would have happened to me without Rohini.

When Rohini comes home next time, I would like to introduce Jiya to her. Rohini got married before I met Jiya. A few days later Rohini came home with her husband for the weekend. I introduced her to Jiya. Rohini was very happy talking to Jiya. While returning to her in-laws home after spending the weekend, Rohini told me, "If you want to marry Jiya, don't listen to anyone's objections, Jiya really loves you." Why did Rohini say this? Did she hunch something?

Some more time passed by. Jiya had just got a job at a college. After that, there was no difficulty in getting married. But none of us could tell that at home. There must be objections from my house about Jiya's employment. And it happened.
My parents said one more thing, "The girl is Sunil's friend, right?"
"Yes, but what happened to that?"
"Are you sure she loves you and not Sunil?"
"Sunil is only her friend, nothing more. I know right."
"We have seen Jiya many times, albeit from a distance, but we think she likes Sunil. They are very good friends."
"Yes. Exactly. They are only friends."
"And besides that she works in a college. Is she willing to leave it?"
I didn't feel like talking anymore. I was very tired. I said to them, "Let's drop it, I will not marry anyone."

After that, all of us were very upset. I hadn't talked to anyone properly for a few days. After a few days, one day I saw Sunil come to our house. I didn't want to talk to anyone, so I was going to leave the room. Sunil called me. After that Sunil talked to me for some time. What Sunil said was that he and Jiya liked each other from the beginning. But after meeting me, Jiya used to keep a little distance from Sunil. Sunil was very upset, but did not say anything to Jiya. But he thinks that Jiya might like Sunil till date. He felt that I had helped Jiya and her family a lot, so Jiya couldn't say no to my marriage proposal.

"No, no, no. I do not believe this at all. I have to talk to Jiya about this." I said to myself, but I didn't say anything to Sunil. But before talking to Jiya I called my sister Rohini. Rohini told me that Sunil is not talking right at all. My sister believes, if Jiya really loves anyone, it is only Rishav and no one else. This is exactly my thought. But before marriage maybe I should talk about this.

Jiya and I were walking around one day. I told Jiya, "My parents don't agree to this marriage."
"So what to do now?"
"Then what else, you marry someone else, I too have to marry any girl my parents like"
"Well. Then you want to marry another girl. You could have said that directly. Why blame the parents? They will never force you to marry someone you don't like."
"Why?"
"Tell me one thing, can you be happy living your whole life away from the one you truly love? Or, can you spend the rest of your life with someone you don't love at all?"
"Then why are you marrying me?"
"What kinda question is this? How can I stay away from you my whole life?"

"Why?"

"Why are you asking such strange questions today?"

"I just wanted to hear that I love you. How much you talked, but you didn't say it even once."

"I love you, Rishav. That's why I've decided to marry you."

"Do you really love me, and no one else, Jiya?"

"Who else can be?"

"I don't know that. You know if you love someone else."

"I don't know either."

"Shall I find out?"

"Let it be. You don't need to do that much, Rishav."

"Otherwise you have to marry me."

"How many times do I have to say that I love you and I want to marry only you and no one else?"

After coming back home that day I told my parents that I want to marry Jiya. After that, quite some months passed. They were not agreeable at first but eventually accepted everything for my happiness.

Some small memories of our wedding and some rituals come to my mind even today. On your wedding day, everyone smeared a lot of turmeric on me. Four old friends of mine had just told me earlier, "Today morning you will be marionetted well with turmeric, then you will be roasted during the rituals and Jiya will eat you tonight." Later, after a few hours, they told me with a smile, "Don't play music loudly today, Jiya doesn't like it.

If you play loud music, your marriage may be annulled." Our wedding day was full of such small candied moments. Jiya came to our house with me as my wife. When entering the house, my parents and relatives all blessed us. From that day we both started walking together as each other's life partner. We did not realize then that the road ahead of us in life would be so difficult.

The days after marriage were very beautiful. Back home, Jiya tried to learn various types of housework from my mother. Jiya loved to sing, paint, and handle office work. My Jiya was never interested in those household chores. But she used to try hard to do these things because she wanted to see a little smile on my parents' faces. She could not do any work properly. Many mistakes had been made by her every day. And all the anger of my parents fell on Jiya's job. They always said, "Jiya is married now, so she should quit her job and focus on her home."

Due to family objections, Jiya quit her job and started her own business. But this also did not work. Even after our marriage Sunil used to come home sometimes to meet my parents. But Jiya was not at home then. One day I returned a little while ago and Sunil was there at my home. Seeing me, Sunil said, "You have come home, but Jiya is not back yet."
I replied, "She will come when her work is done."

Sunil said, "A married girl has some responsibilities at home too. And your parents don't like Jiya's job at all."
I told Sunil, "You don't worry so much about these things."

Then Sunil went home. But after Jiya returned, the atmosphere in the house became completely silent. From then on it happened sometimes. I thought our relationship would be better if we stay apart from your parents. When I said this at home, Jiya went crazy with happiness like a little girl. But my parents were very upset. They did not say anything but were completely silent. I thought everything would be fine after a few days, maybe my parents would accept Jiya's work. But it didn't happen.

Jiya and I started living in the new apartment. Then Sunil started helping in Jiya's business. I did not like some things about Sunil. I did not want Sunil to join Jiya's business. But later I came to know that Sunil was helping Jiya a lot. I was very happy that Jiya could spend more time at home. At that time a maid is kept at home so that we can spend more time together. But no. That didn't happen anymore. Sometimes I would come back home and see that Jiya did not return. I was waiting for her then. Sometimes I called my friends. Sometimes at home. Talked with my parents. My parents knew many things about Jiya's business, which Jiya never told me. My parents could know everything from Sunil. Jiya wanted to grow the business very quickly. Sunil repeatedly requested her not to do so much work in one day, he every day requested her to return home early, but Jiya did not listen. Jiya used to say that she doesn't like to return home early. There was no need to rush as there was a maid at home. Sunil used to tell her to go home and spend time with Rishav. Jiya used to say, "I don't like to go back home. You understand business more, you understand me more, Rishav doesn't want to understand me at all."

Oh God, Jiya could think like that! These words broke my heart every day. But looking at Jiya's ocean eyes, I didn't want to believe that my Jiya could say such a thing. But can't Jiya sometimes return home a little early? Does she not want to remember me at least once a day in her busy time? The conversation between us was very less. Sometimes I was very sad. I used to go to bed without having dinner. After coming home, when Jiya got to know that I had fallen asleep without eating, she also used to fall asleep without eating dinner, but she never said to me, "Let's have dinner together tonight." I was missing my old Jiya so much. Did Jiya miss me like that? From my heart, I wanted to get back to that old time. Does Jiya want the same? Maybe she thought. So after a few days, I noticed that she used to come back home a little early. I wanted to say many things to Jiya then, but there was a distance between us. And Sunil's words that he told my parents? Are those true? I felt we should spend some time together, away from all the work. In solitude. But I had a doubt, "Will Jiya agree?" Let's see. I had planned to celebrate our anniversary in Goa. I texted Jiya. Jiya had an important meeting that day, but Jiya's reply came immediately. Out of happiness, I felt like running away to Goa immediately holding Jiya's hand. I couldn't wait any longer. On the day of our departure for Goa, Sunil came to the airport to get Jiya's signature on some papers. But he came so late that Jiya did not have time to look at those papers. Who knows what papers Jiya signed? It was too late that day, so I didn't like to think about these things.

The next five days were so beautiful that it felt like we were in paradise. Even before my marriage, I came to visit Goa along with my four close friends. But Goa never seemed so beautiful before.

Five days just flew away. We returned home with a heart full of joy. Then we did not understand that time would change so soon. After coming back from Goa, Jiya became very quiet. What happened to her? Was she not happy? She became slightly absent-minded. She didn't talk to me well, always thinking about something. Was there any problem occurring in her business? I suddenly remembered that Sunil used to share a lot with my parents. My parents might know if she was facing any kind of problem at work or not. Talking to my parents, I came to know that Sunil's father was very sick in the

village. Jiya was very worried about that. But for him, Jiya would do this to me? Anyway, I called Sunil to inquire about his father's health. I came to a standstill hearing what Sunil told me. Has Sunil gone crazy? What was Sunil saying? Or, was his every word true? I yelled at Sunil, "Shut up. What are you saying?"
Sunil replied in a very calm tone, "I have all the proof of what I am saying. Do you want to see it? Then I will send all the evidence to your office address. Just message me the address" Sunil immediately disconnected the call after saying this.

Can close people change so quickly, or are there no such things as close people in this world?

4

A small tidy house in Kalkaji, South Delhi. The single-storey house, the second floor was under construction. Some flower plants were planted in front of the house. Many more beautiful houses were being built next to the house. The front house is very beautiful. It was already made many years ago. People lived there. Uncle Ranajit and Aruna of that house loved me very much. No. They were not our relatives, our neighbours. I respectfully called them uncle and aunt. Their children were very good at their studies. They were older than me, so I didn't have much friendship with them. I used to go to their house only to talk to uncle Ranajit and aunt Aruna. Aunt Aruna fondly called me Sonu. How much affection there was in this name, just hearing the call from her filled my heart with happiness.

I came to Delhi with my mother from the village when I was only nine years old and studying in the fourth standard. Dad used to live here long ago. As the second floor was under construction, I was not allowed to move to that floor. So after coming from school, I used to play alone in our garden, or I used to go to the house in front. Slowly our second floor was ready, but I didn't stop going to that house of those uncle and aunt. I had many friends at school, one of them came to our house sometimes. I used to walk around a lot in the afternoon with my friends. The more I got to know Delhi, the more I began to like the city. But after going to the tenth standard that year, the outdoor movements had to be reduced a bit. Then I focused on studies. Sometimes I used to study together at our house, sometimes at my friends' house. A few days after the tenth standard started, one day I saw a new girl in the class. The girl was newly admitted to this school. She could talk a lot. My friend Arushi and that girl quickly became very good friends. After some time I became very good friends with that girl because of Aarushi. Her name is Jiya. We three friends used to study together, sometimes going here and there in the twilight. Suddenly one day I heard a loud voice in front of my house. It was Jiya's voice. Is Jiya in any danger? Why is she shouting so loudly? Hearing her voice, I came downstairs. What I saw when I came down made me laugh. Stifling my chuckle, I brought Jiya and Rishav inside the room. Jiya didn't want to stay longer and left soon that day. Jiya did not like Rishav at all. Very good. Rishav and his sister Rohini were a bit self-conceited as they were very good at studies. I used to go to their house since I came from the village. That front house. Their parents Ranajit and Aruna loved me, but Rishav and Rohini did not talk to me much. My friend Jiya was also very good at studies. But still how nicely she used to talk to me. I really like this sweet behavior of Jiya.

I was very busy with studies. The final exam was ahead. At that time our group study was reduced a lot. Meetings with Jiya and Arushi were rare. One day I had a headache after studying for 7-8 hours at a stretch. I thought I would go out and have tea from a nearby tea stall, a little walk would be done with it. I went out and saw Jiya and Rishav walking together. I was surprised to see that. Since when did this happen? The next morning I called Jiya and Arushi and said, "I have some questions, I want to study together." They came that evening. While studying, I brought up the topic of Rishav several times. Jiya did not get angry after hearing Rishav's name that day, and was silent. Sometimes I don't understand Jiya at all. Since when my friend had changed so much, I could not know anything? I cannot put into words how much pain I felt that day. And I don't know why I got so angry with Jiya. But I could not say anything, I was completely silent. I wanted to tell Jiya never to talk to Rishav further. But why would Jiya listen if I say this? So I was very upset. I wanted to lose neither Jiya nor Arushi, they are very good friends of mine. But why did this friendship between Jiya and Rishav bother me so much? Even after the final exam, the three of us used to meet, sometimes we would go for a walk. Our friendship was the same as before. Then we got admitted in the same institution in the eleventh class. I was very happy to have Jiya and Arushi again as classmates. Rishav was studying engineering far away. He used to come home after many days. I thought that

Jiya and Rishav's friendship might not last long. I was very happy thinking about this. Jiya never said a word about Rishav. Sometimes I used to ask Jiya if she had any talk with Rishav. Jiya replied, "What should I talk about with him?" I was overjoyed to hear this.

Before the completion of my studies I had to join my father's business. The business was running at a loss at that time. My father and I were working hard to fix everything. My contact with everything except business greatly reduced. But despite all our efforts, we could not save anything. My father's business started crumbling gradually. I was also very broken inside. I had a lot of dreams, which also kept falling apart one by one along with the business. A few years passed like a nightmare. Leaving only our home in Delhi, the three of us returned to our village in Odisha. Went to visit Ranjit uncle and Aruna aunty in the front house before leaving for our village. I also thought of meeting Arushi and Jiya before leaving. It had been a long time since we last spoke properly. But when I went to Rishav's house and heard the news from his mother, aunt Aruna, I became mad with anger. Our business, my love, all ended at a time. I returned home quietly. I then avoided entering my mother's room. How to tell my mom that Rishav and Jiya were going to get married very soon. My mother could understand how much I love Jiya. The news of their marriage must be kept secret from my mother. But my mom came to know this from other neighbours. And what I feared happened. Mom started to cry, taking me in her arms. I couldn't hold myself back then, and started crying a lot.

We returned to our village. At that time I had no money, my heart was empty, I was in a frenzy. I used to sit at home all day totally silent. In the evening I usually went to the riverside and sat alone leaning against a tree. If I was very angry, I would throw stones one after another into the river. And I felt the exact same sound deep in my heart that came out of the river after throwing stones.

One day I was sitting at home, then mom came and sat next to me. I was so deep in thought that I didn't notice at first. I was startled when mother gently took my hand and gave me the food plate.
"When did you come?" I asked
"What do you think about so much all day?" Mom asked me.
"No, nothing. Let's eat together. How long have we not eaten together? Mom, where is dad?"
"Your father went outside to look for some work. No matter what, we have to run the family."
"Why did everything finish like this, mom?"
"Nothing is finished. Don't say this at all. You are there. You will rebuild everything again. I have faith in you. You must. Either way, you have to do it."
"Definitely. That's what I was thinking, how to bring everything back."

"Why don't you go to Delhi and meet Aruna once? Called you two days ago. You were not at home. We talked a lot."

"Yes, you are right, mom. She loves me very much. I should go someday."

After a few days I went to their house. Rishav and Jiya's wedding is ahead. I asked aunt Aruna, "Has Jiya agreed to leave her job?"

She replied very upset, "No. Boys and girls in recent days don't obey their parents anymore. They follow their own rules. Our words have no value to them anymore."

I was surprised and asked aunt Aruna, "Then why did you agree to this marriage? Just say no. My bro Rishav is a very good guy. If you do not agree, Rishav will never marry Jiya. You should rather find another good girl for Rishav. He will surely like that girl."

I kept on convincing her again and again that they should not allow Rishav's marriage with Jiya. But Rishav and her sister Rohini together already spoke to their parents about this. Rohini is married and still employed. Even if their house didn't approve, Rohini fully supported Rishav's marriage with Jiya. What else could be done? I also tried to talk to Rishav to stop that marriage, but all in vain.

There was very little land adjacent to our little house in the village. There we made a small kitchen garden. One morning my mother and I were working there and just then uncle Ranajit's phone came. He talked with my father. He invited us to Rishav's wedding. O Lord, Rishav would marry my Jiya in front of my eyes, how could I see it? This marriage would happen. And breaking my heart that marriage took place. Only my father attended Rishav's wedding. My mother and I went to their house after a few months. Jiya and Rishav were not at home at that time, they were at their office. Jiya involved herself in various cultural activities after taking classes at her college. Usually she was too late to return home. Then she had to study a lot after coming back home. My mother and I provoked aunt Aruna a lot to create trouble between Jiya and Rishav. Especially about Jiya's job. I knew Jiya would never leave her job and stay at home. The only matter was if Rishav didn't support it. Then surely there will be misunderstanding between them. And so happened. At times Rishav was completely silent on this inquietude of the house. He directly stopped supporting his wife in front of his parents. But my Jiya was a real fighter. She was not a woman to give up on anything. Jiya quit her job at the request of her parents-in-law, but she set up her new business. I always wanted to break Jiya, her relationship with Rishav, but my Jiya kept rebuilding herself and broke my spirit every time.

Once I got a very good opportunity. Jiya, the only daughter-in-law of the house, could not attend her parents-in-law's wedding anniversary. That day Rohini was also a little angry with Jiya, but did not say anything.

I repeatedly explained to uncle Ranajit and aunt Aruna that Jiya should get a befitting punishment for this. They were already very upset with Jiya, so they agreed with me. But Rishav and Jiya's love defeated me once again. Jiya and Rishav decided to leave their house together.

No, it couldn't be done that way. Something should have to be done between Rishav and Jiya. But what would I do? The bond of love between them was very strong. For that, I would have to get close to Jiya. But how? I would have to do something before they go to their new home. I used to go to aunt Aruna and cry again and again for our condition. I told her that I was trying hard to get a job. One day I asked aunt Aruna, "Shall I ask Jiya to give me a chance to work in her business? I have worked with my father before. I have experience. But there is only one problem, Jiya is a very good friend of mine, a very good woman, she will never agree to be my boss."
Aunt Aruna was very happy to hear this and said, "You don't need to worry, if you agree to work with her, I will talk to Jiya about it."
What else would I want? Exactly what I wanted, happened.

My blueprint is ready. Now it's just a matter of implementation. And I would do that. Jiya is a very good girl, but very ambitious. She would not compromise on her work. She must be dealt with very carefully. If I could

once bring Jiya's empire into my hands, Jiya would also be mine. Ha ha ha.... Everything would be mine.
Now, I would take over everything slowly. I only needed a little patience to break the love of Jiya and Rishav. I kept going according to my plan. I joined Jiya's business. After looking at all the documents little by little, I understood everything very quickly. After this, I should become Jiya's trusted secretary. For that I needed the help of some reliable people. I met many people while handling my father's business. Help can be taken from some of them. I was planning how to proceed step by step. They all helped me a lot. Every time I made a few of them as clients and introduced them to Jiya. I always tried to keep her very busy, so that she would go home very late. I used to arrange client meetings with her lots of times, unnecessarily. And I took over the responsibility of handling the legal side of her business. As I had previous experience of running an atelier, she trusted me and gave me this responsibility. I made her trade as well as her life a mockery. But there were also some real clients for whom the business was running smoothly. Jiya was very happy. I used to keep her busier than she actually should be. Sometimes I used to call Aruna aunt. There was a lot of talk. I also mentioned that Jiya works way more than necessary to grow her business even faster. Aunt was sad. Aunt was saddened thinking that Jiya is focused only on her business, not on her family. Jiya and Rishav loved each other deeply, so even if they couldn't spend much time with each other,

their love would never fade. I understood that very well. Therefore, to raise the misunderstanding between the two true lovers, my first act was to reduce their communication. I started to think, what could be done for this. And then an opportunity came.

One day Rishav himself called me after talking to his mother, my aunt Aruna. He asked about the health of my parents. Then inquired about the business. But did not ask anything directly. I was asked, how did I feel about working in Jiya's business?

I said, "Business is going very well. Jiya takes very good care of everything. I am an ordinary employee, but she takes so much care for me too. Apart from business, Jiya also spends a lot of quality time with me. It's a matter of luck to have a boss like Jiya. Jiya is your life partner, she surely spends more beautiful time with you."

"Yes, of course she does." Saying this, Rishav hung up the phone.

After that sometimes I called Rishav, and Rishav called me too. As much as I could, I exaggerated everything, especially about the moments Jiya and I used to spend together. One day I was talking to Rishav. While talking, I said to Rishav, "Jiya doesn't want to go home early these days. So maybe she keeps herself more busy with work. I try to convince Jiya a lot, so that she returns home soon, but she doesn't listen to me. Jiya told me that she prefers to be in the office than at home, and it gives her the opportunity to spend a lot of time with me." "Well, I have another important call." Saying this, Rishav disconnected the call again.

Jiya had to sign many business documents. Before signing I checked everything carefully and then took it to the lawyer and got those papers ready. After that, Jiya checked and then signed those papers. At first Jiya used to check everything before signing. Seeing that I did all the work perfectly, Jiya's trust in me increased a lot. After that I started to keep Jiya busy in meetings more and more. As a result Jiya was running out of time to scrutinize all the documents. After that I kept on convincing Jiya more and more that she should spend more time with Rishav. Rishav may feel lonely without her. I used to explain to Jiya, "You sign today and go home, Rishav needs you, take a lot of time tomorrow and check those papers properly. Sign it before going home so I can go to the lawyer if required. Then I don't need to bother you if you are busy with the morning meeting."

Jiya signed many documents which were very useful for me. Jiya never got a chance to verify those papers. Slowly, Jiya was signing many such things. But suddenly, one day, Jiya really pissed me off. Jiya and Rishav planned to get closer to each other. They were going to Goa to spend five days together, just the two of them. Thus they would reduce misapprehension with each other. I had to do something. Only two more days were left. Everything must be done within it. But what could I do so quickly, how to do it? But something must be done. Talked to the lawyer Jatin. Once I introduced him to Jiya. He looked after the legal side of Jiya's business, but he didn't talk much directly with Jiya. I used to deal with legal matters for a long time, so he used to talk to me. He prepared all the documents as I wanted. And he was known to me for a long time. I informed him that everything was being done with Jiya's consent and I produced all the documents signed by Jiya as evidence. After that I continued to deal with the lawyer and later he got to know everything and helped me enough to do my work. Only he could help me at this point. I told him everything and said that the whole thing should be completed within two days.

He said, "Everything will be done. Just some documents will require Jiya's signature. Either way, it has to be done without letting Jiya understand anything."

Everything was ready in two days. It was pre-planned, so I was preparing everything. That work had been completed in just two days. After that all it needed was Jiya's signature on it. But Jiya would want to take a good look. How could it have been prevented? No matter. This should be done on the day they were leaving. So Jiya won't have time to see them at all. The night before their departure, I called Jiya and said that Jiya had missed signing some documents. If Jiya doesn't sign them, I won't be able to proceed with the client meeting. Hearing this, Jiya was very worried. I assured her that I would go to the airport the next day to get her signature and get the whole thing done. Then Jiya was quite convinced.

the next day. Jiya and Rishav reached the airport very early. Then Jiya was calling me again and again. Everything must be checked and signed. So she was in a hurry. But that should not be allowed to happen. Jiya would sign but won't have time to verify. I left home early to go to the airport. But instead of going to the airport, I sat at a restaurant. I took a lot of time and had breakfast there. Meanwhile, Jiya was continuously making calls. I told her that the car had broken down on the road, so it was taking some time. It would only take four to five minutes to sign. I would Just have to give that little bit of time. If she gets more time, Jiya would check the papers.

I was too late to get there. My Jiya was very angry with me. Only a few days left. After that, this angry girl would become completely mine. Then I will slowly break all the anger of the girl with a lot of time. I had arranged everything. I was thinking to myself, "Go Jiya, spend a few days happily with your Rishav for the last time. After this you will not get this opportunity in life, I will separate you and Rishav forever and then you will be only mine."

After somehow signing, the angry girl went inside the airport. She didn't say a single word to me while leaving. When Jiya left, I sat outside the airport for a long time. After looking at the papers carefully, I hugged them. These are no longer just pieces of paper, these are the key to bringing Jiya to me. I was very excited. I thought how soon those five days would pass and my Jiya would come back to me. Then I won't let Jiya stay close to Rishav for too long. I need to get her as soon as possible.

I walked out of the airport. Five days later Jiya returned to Delhi. The next day she came to the office and wanted to see all the documents. Everything was ready. I did not present all the papers. I then reminded her that I had to go to the lawyer first with these papers. Some work was yet to be done. Jiya agreed. Said to finish the pending work first. She would wait for me till I finish the work and come back to the office. Without further delay, I went out with everything. First I went to the lawyer. After seeing all the documents, he said, "Everything is correctly done. The arrangement is perfect."
I gave him the rest of his fee and said, "I won't be late. I'm out now. Jiya might call you. You'll handle it."
He smiled and said, "All your work will be done. Go, now. Otherwise you'll be late."

I left and got on the train. Another advantage was that the station was not far from the lawyer's house. I arrived early. I did not return to the office that day, I went back to our village. After that I informed Jiya very late that my father suddenly felt very ill in the village. I had no choice but to leave for my village immediately. I told her that I had taken all the papers in the file with me, and I would return to Delhi within a week. But then I would not go back to Delhi. I kept being late. Meanwhile, Jiya was getting restless. I also informed aunt Aruna about my father's deteriorating health. And it worked. Rishav did not want to listen to a single word about me from Jiya. Rishav called me after hearing about my father's illness from his mother. Talked to him for a long time. I told Rishav about our love. Jiya and me. Told him how much we love each other.

Rishav said, "Stop your nonsense. I don't believe any of this."

I said, "Believe me Rishav, Jiya doesn't want to be with you anymore. She is very worried about my father's health. So she doesn't talk to you much these days. Jiya has promised me that she will leave you and come to me as soon as I return to Delhi."

Rishav threatened me, "Jiya will never leave me and go to you."

"Rishav, Jiya will come to me. Take my word for it. Jiya has not only promised me, she has given me something more."

"And what is that?"

"Proof. Proof that she will come to me."
"Tell me, what proof did Jiya give you?"
"Proof that she really loves me."
"Shut up. What are you saying?"
"I have all the proof of what I am saying. Do you want to see it? Then I will send all the evidence to your office address. Just message me the address.".

A few minutes after receiving Rishav's message, I called uncle Ranajit. Aunt Aruna answered the call. I cried a lot and said that my father's health had deteriorated further. She was very sad to hear that. After talking to her I immediately switched off my phone. Then I sent all the papers to Rishav's office. I had prepared one copy of all the documents beforehand. These should reach Rishav properly. After that I would have no worries. Rishav would do the rest of my work with these papers. I won't have to do anything else. Jiya would come to me then.

I began to feel as if the whole world is mine, the whole kingdom is mine, the princess is mine. I went crazy with happiness.

5

Today, on the first anniversary of our mom's death, sitting in front of her picture, my brother Rishav and I could not hold back the tears. This photo was taken on my parents' wedding anniversary. How beautiful everything was then. Mom is smiling sweetly in the photo. After that our family was torn apart for just one person. My mom left with so much pain.

My brother got up silently and stood on the balcony. Dad was sitting silently on a chair in front of our mother's photo. None of us have seen my brother's offspring. No one knows where Jiya went after having the baby. Rishav took his transfer to Bangalore after a few months of their separation. He left Delhi and started living in Bangalore. After Jiya and Rishav got separated, our parents were very hurt. My mother used to be very upset. My mother loved Sunil very much, lovingly named him Sonu. And then Rishav's family was broken for her Sonu. Exactly 1 year and 8 months after Rishav and Jiya's separation, my mother died suddenly. Rishav came from Bangalore. Our father became all alone at home in Delhi. After our mother's death, Rishav decided to sell his and Jiya's dream house in Delhi. But after going there everything changed. Rishav thought to bring all the necessary things and files from their house. He suddenly discovered a medical file of Jiya in it. There were some test reports of Jiya which proved that she was two months pregnant at the time of their separation. Rishav immediately took the file and visited the doctor whom Jiya was consulting. He talked to her doctor. Then the doctor's PA searched the old appointment book and informed Rishav that Jiya came there till the 6th month of her pregnancy. Then where did Jiya go? From the doctor's clinic Rishav went to Jiya's parental house in Delhi. Another family was then staying in the house where Jiya lived with her parents. Rishav was very broken when he found no trace of Jiya. She could not be reached by phone. Maybe Jiya's phone number had changed. And just then their old neighbour informed him that Jiya had returned to their home in Chandigarh with her mother after her father's death. She was 6 months pregnant at that time. Then Rishav called me and our father from there to tell everything. Oh God! None of us can forget the day when we got the news of their child's birth. A terrible disaster happened that day. From jiya's rented apartment in Delhi, Rishav immediately left for Chandigarh by driving. That night we repeatedly requested him to go the next morning, but he did not listen to anyone. Our mother passed away just a few days before that. The grief of mother's death, the pain of being away from his child, Rishav was not in a position to make any decision then. My brother was driving to Chandigarh from Delhi that night. By any means, he wanted to reach Jiya as early as possible. Was Sunil with her? Don't know. But Rishav was driving at a very high speed to Jiya. Before he reached there, the accident happened on the highway. None of us knew then. In the morning we called Rishav again and again, but Rishav did not pick up. Then we started looking for Rishav. After much searching, he was found that evening. At a hospital. Was in the ICU. Fatal accident. The doctor said he may not survive his bad condition. During the accident, his phone was lost somewhere, no one could find it anywhere, so our calls remained unanswered. After a 3 month fight with death my brother recovered and returned from the hospital. Even after returning home from the hospital, it took another 3 months for Rishav to fully recover. At that time, none of us could search for Jiya. When we again started searching after Rishav's recovery, there was no trace of Jiya. Did Jiya really go to Sunil? I couldn't believe this at all. I don't think my brother believes this either. But Sunil sent proof to my brother Rishav. Can people really change so much? However, none of us know where Sunil and Jiya are now. I know my brother is still looking for Jiya.

When we find someone who is far away, it feels like the world is so small, we can find anyone we want. On the other hand, when a loved one goes missing, and cannot be found after many attempts, then this world seems much larger in size than billions of universes. No one other than the sufferer can only understand how deeply a heart breaks when a loved one disappears or changes without letting anyone understand. When I see my brother Rishav smiling with a broken heart, I can't control my tears. He was absolutely silent. Then he was slowly getting better. After our mom's death, I did not understand how to console my father and brother. My father was alone then. So my husband and I brought my father to our new house in Karol Bagh. Delhi railway station is not too far from here. My son and daughter study in a reputed school nearby. My father spends his whole day happily with them when they come back from school.

It has been more than two and half years since Jiya and Rishav separated. I still want Jiya to come back, for everything to be the way it was before. But I can't say that to anyone. My brother doesn't live here anymore, dad will be upset if I tell him this.

I was sitting quietly on the balcony on a Sunday afternoon. My son and daughter went to my in-law's house with my husband Manish. Today I did not go with them because I wanted to spend some time talking with my father. After lunch, father is now resting a little in his room. Sitting on the balcony I was reading a book. A lawyer's house is next to our house. That lawyer, Jatin, is an old friend of Manish. They lived in that house for many years. He helped us get this house. There are very beautiful flowers in the garden in front of his house. While reading the book, my eyes kept going in that direction. His wife takes good care of their garden. Suddenly a bike stopped in front of their house. I know very well the man who took off his helmet and entered their house. I was shocked to see the man. Sunil. What is he doing here? Why did Sunil go to that house? Does Jatin know Sunil? After about an hour, Sunil left Jatin's house. I did not talk to my father about this. When Manish returned home, I told him everything. Manish said Jatin is a lawyer. Sunil must be his client. Manish guessed exactly right. We were all stunned to hear everything from Jatin. Jatin is a professional lawyer. He didn't want to say anything at first. But we told him everything that happened in my brother's life. Manish told him, "We just want to know where Rishav's wife Jiya is. Is she really with Sunil now? Our only concern is Jiya."

Jatin was surprised, "Why will Jiya stay with Sunil? Although Sunil had been trying to get her for many years.

In order to get Jiya, and rebuild Sunil's father's old business, Sunil cheated Jiya for a long time and slowly took everything from her to his own name. For this, Sunil first merged their old business with Jiya's Business. Then one by one he started transferring everything of Jiya to his own name. And he did all this without letting Jiya understand anything. He did this very cleverly, and Jiya always kept on believing him."

Hearing all this, once again my heart was filled with love for Jiya and was immediately angry with Sunil. But no. I can't just get angry like this. Something must be done. First of all, these should be said to my brother. He needs to understand that what we apparently see most of the time, may not always be true. I repeatedly told him not to lose faith in Jiya, not to trust Sunil so much. But that time my brother relied only on Sunil's evidence.

There are some people in this world who knowingly lower the dignity of others and create misunderstandings in love relationships for their own benefit, and then destroy those beautiful relationships permanently. Those who break a love relationship ultimately gain nothing, but make the two lovers terribly destitute.

"But Sunil has already grabbed everything of Jiya, what does he want now, what else is left?" I asked Jatin again.

Jatin replied, "Sunil could not gain anything by taking everything away from Jiya. After Jiya left, Sunil could not handle the trade properly. As a result, the business again started running at a loss. Sunil started selling all the assets of the business one by one. Now only the building where Jiya had set up her office remains to be sold."

"So Sunil will sell that office now?" Manish asked this.

"No. It won't be that easy." Jatin replied.

I asked "why?"

Now Jatin gave an important information, "If Sunil wants to sell, he will need the deed, occupancy certificate, tax receipt etc. which are with Jiya."

I called Rishav and told, "There is a very urgent need, come to our house as soon as possible." My brother was very worried after hearing this. But he can't be told anything like this. Slowly I have to explain everything in detail to him. After he came, Manish and I started telling him everything. Rishav was very happy to hear that Jiya is not with Sunil, But then he became restless thinking about where Jiya is now.
I told him, "That is what we have to find out now."
"But where can Jiya be found? She left her house in Chandigarh, no one knows where she went. No one lives in that house now. So how do we get news of Jiya?" Rishav asked.
"Only Sunil might know where Jiya is. But he won't reveal anything" I said to him.
"So what can be done now?" He asked again.
"We have to know everything from sunil. For this, we have to catch him, but without letting him understand." I replied.
Rishav said, "It's impossible. How can we do this?"
"That's what we have to figure out." I answered.

After 12 midnight this locality becomes very quiet, people are not seen on the streets much. Many people have purchased plots here, but many of those are still empty, no houses have been built yet. So the area is quite empty. The houses are quite far from each other. After 8pm, no cars ply here except some private cars. There are few shops here, which are open till 10pm. Then everything gets closed. In some houses people stay up till 12 midnight. After that the whole area seems completely tranquilized.

It's almost 2:30 in the night. The man silently came and stood in front of the house. Then he carefully looked around. He slowly walked around the house once. Checked if everything is fine. Now he stood in front of the main gate and lit the torch once. The street lamp is a little far from this house. So this house looks a bit blurry from a distance. Now the man broke the lock of the door very precisely. He slowly entered the house without making a sound. Once again he lit the torch and looked for the stairs going up. The lock on the upper floor was not very easy to break. But this time also the way he broke the lock, it's clear that the man came well prepared. And without delay, the man hurriedly entered, then closed the door. Lighting the torch, he looked around cautiously. He had been here only once before. That too for a very short time. That time the owners of this house lived here. No one lives here anymore. The interior of the house was very well decorated. But now is not the time to think about this. He has to finish his work quickly. Lighting the torch he entered the first bedroom. There is a large bed, two side tables on either side of the bed and one small two-door cupboard. And a beautifully crafted vanity table. It was not found in this room even after searching all around. From there, he entered another bedroom on the opposite side of the living room. Does this room contain that desired item? This room has a small bed. And two huge wardrobes. Some items are scattered here and there. No, it was not found in this room even after a very good search. Another bedroom is yet to be searched. The man entered the third bedroom. There are not too many things here. Some paintings hang on the wall, a big table with chairs, some books on the table, There is a large mirror that hangs on the wall. Right on the opposite side, there is a picture of the owners of this house. Nothing special to look for here. Only the drawers of the table. No. Nothing's here either. So where is it kept? Is it in the living room? In the kitchen? Where? Where is it kept? Even after a lot of searching, it was found nowhere. So is it not in this house? Surely it is here, otherwise where will it go? Entering the third bedroom again, the man kept his hands on the table and sat on the chair thinking. While thinking, the man's eyes went towards that big mirror again. House owners' pictures on the opposite side of the mirror looked very beautiful. He lit the torch and saw that photo again and again. Suddenly the man felt like throwing the picture and breaking it. Once again he felt like breaking the mirror. He lit the torch and placed it on the table, then went to the mirror. Angrily, the man removed the mirror from the wall. When he was about to break, he noticed a small door behind the mirror. Quickly putting the mirror down, the man started searching for its key. While looking for that, the man might have seen that there are some keys in the drawer of the table. Yes, that's right. Taking out the keys from there, the man hurriedly tried to open the lock with one key after another. Now the lock opened with a creaking sound when a key was turned. There are several files inside it, and a box. The man fetched the torch from the table and started searching madly. First he opened the box. Some jewellery is kept here. Nothing more. He decided to take those with him. But before that, he needs to find the file. Here it is. Yes, that's it. The man came out quickly with File and the jewellery box. He hurried down the stairs and came out through the main gate. As soon as he came out and stood up, a strong light came into the man's eyes. The man closed his eyes in the light.

Entering inside the Jyoti Nagar police station, Rishav couldn't control his anger, grabbing the collar of the handcuffed man he asked, "Sunil, you have to tell me, why did you harm us like this?" Manish and I somehow pacified Rishav. Then he sat in the front chair. I explained to Rishav, "Sunil has no way to escape. He has been caught red-handed stealing Jiya's jewellery and the deed of her office property."
Sunil shouted, "My lawyer told me that Deed may be at Jiya's house. Take that Deed from there. I just did as he

said. Here's no fault of mine. I want to talk to my lawyer first."

Jatin, his lawyer, was present there. He scolded Sunil and said, "I just said that you must need the deed to sell the office, it can be at Jiya's house, bring it from her. I never told you to steal it."

I said to Sunil, "You were told knowingly that Deed is in Jiya's house. I requested Jatin to tell you this. I knew you were desperate, you'd steal it. And not only the Deed, you are also caught stealing Jiya's jewellery. While sending you the message that the deed is at their house, we had replaced the original with a copy."

Then my brother Rishav burst into tears. Sobbing he said to Sunil, "Do you have any idea of what you have done for your greed? You separated me from Jiya, separated me from my child. I could not see my own child's face till today because of you. And what do you get by doing this much? Jiya never loved you, so she didn't go to you even when she was alone. And you cheated Jiya and took away her business to get her but couldn't save this business either."

I said, "Really Sunil, this is what I really want to know, what did you get by doing this? Why did you tell Rishav that Jiya loves you, and as a proof of that love, Jiya has written everything in your name. Jiya never really loved you, you just cheated her. You created such a misunderstanding between Rishav and Jiya that Jiya could not even tell Rishav about her pregnancy. Even when Jiya needed her husband the most, Jiya was alienated by Rishav."

Gaurav was listening to everything silently. Now he said, "Rohini, Rishav, don't worry, Sunil will be punished for everything he has done."
Rishav's childhood friend Gaurav is now the inspector of Jyoti Nagar police station. Sunil could not have been caught without his help.
I said to Gaurav, "First of all we need to know about Jiya from Sunil. Is she fine? Where is she?"
Now Sunil replied, "I really don't know where Jiya is. I switched off my phone after sending Rishav a copy of all the signed documents of Jiya's business. I knew Jiya would be very angry with me, and would try to contact me. After several months, I thought that Jiya's anger on me might have decreased. So I tried to contact her many times. She didn't talk to me. I couldn't even find her on social media. Unable to contact Jiya, I contacted our friend Arushi on a social media site. Even Arushi did not reply to me. So I think Jiya told Arushi everything. Try to contact Arushi. She may know where Jiya is."

6

Today is Saturday, weekend, school holiday, so Ronit keeps insisting me to take him to the nearest park. Ron has made several friends here. He wants to go to the park to play with them. But today I will go to meet that man in the evening. That stranger, who seems very close, but I don't know him. I said to my mother, "Please go to the park today with Ron. I have a little work to do, so I have to go out." My mother's health has not been well since the last few days, but I still had to make this request. Otherwise Ron will not want to sit at home in the evening.

I checked the phone while working. That guy sent a message. He wrote, "If your son doesn't want to stay at home today, surely bring him with you. I'd love to talk with him."
Does this guy know telepathy or not? How could he know that Ron would insist on going out with me? Anyway, it's good. My mother can rest at home then, and I won't feel awkward in front of a stranger if Ron is with me. And if Ron is there, I will get an excuse to come home early. I don't want to talk to strangers these days. But once upon a time I used to talk too much. Thinking how much I have changed now, I replied to that guy, "Yes, definitely I'll take Ron with me."
The man was very happy to hear this.

Will leave at 5 pm. I prepared Ron and started getting ready. And I kept thinking, "Will the man come? I'm going to meet a stranger like this, am I doing right?" I went out with Ron thinking about this.

Exactly 5:30 pm, I reached the coffee shop with Ron. I came and messaged the guy, "I've arrived. Where are you?"
"I'm almost there, 2 more minutes," came the reply.
My son was not ready to sit here. He thought he would go to the park today. Ordered some food for Ron and I kept waiting.

Just 2 minutes later I was startled to see the man walking in front of me with a slight limp. I am so surprised that I can't even say anything. This person is not a stranger to me, he is the closest person in my life, who one day pushed me too far. I immediately stood up, I pulled Ron and proceeded to go out. The man folded his hands in front of me apologetically and said, "Please don't leave without listening to me. I have been waiting for this day for a long time. I know you are very angry with me, but forgive me today, listen to me please."
"But I don't want to hear anything from you."
"Jiya, please let me talk to my child."
"Who is your child, Rishav? Ronit is only my son. You pushed both of us away before he came into this world."
"I made a mistake, Jiya, a very big mistake."

"Why did you hide your identity and met me? I would never have talked to you if I had known this before."

"For that, Jiya, only for that. If I were to introduce myself earlier, you would never talk to me, never meet me. Listen to me, Jiya. Please don't go away angry with me today. Then I will lose my whole world forever."

"You already lost that long ago, Rishav. Don't waste my time by saying anything for no reason. You ruined my life long ago. Not anymore."

Now Rishav held my hands and said, "Don't go, Jiya. I have been punished a lot for my mistakes. Don't punish me anymore."

"What did you get punished for? Only I got all the pain. You drove me away, I didn't leave of my own accord. That day I was waiting for your return home. I wanted to let you know about my pregnancy. I thought you would be very happy. You didn't even give me a chance to say this, and all you did was to push me away without hearing anything."

"Is being away from you for so long any less of a punishment? To be away from my own child, was it not an extreme punishment for me?"

"It was entirely your decision to stay away from us, Rishav."

"I misunderstood you Jiya. When I saw you had transferred your business to Sunil's name, your signature was there, seeing that, I could no longer distrust Sunil."

"That day you did not want to listen to me, Rishav. So why are you asking me to listen to you today?"

"Don't make me suffer from being away from you anymore, Jiya."

"When you came inside the cafe, your walk didn't seem normal to me, what happened, Rishav?"

"I'll tell you everything one by one, that's why I came to you, Jiya. First you sit down please, then I shall say everything."

I was very sad. I went and sat quietly with Ron. Rishav followed us and sat on the chair in front.

We were both hesitating, and couldn't understand how to start the conversation.

Then Rishav broke the silence and asked us, "What would you like to order? Will you take coffee? What will Ronit take?"

"Don't worry, I have already ordered some food for Ronit."

Then we both ordered coffee and some snacks.

Now Ron didn't want to sit there. At first he looked at Rishav surprisingly, then insisted on returning home. Then Rishav pulled Ron close to himself. Rishav now hugged Ron. He brought many gifts for Ron and continued to give him one by one. Ron was very happy to receive gifts. Sitting next to Rishav, Ron unwrapped all the presents and started playing with them. Ronit's food was served in between. Now my son got very busy with gifts and food, he forgot to go home.

Rishav again started saying, "You must be very well now, Jiya?"

"I have settled here now. I spend my days busy with Ron and my mother. Nothing more than that. You are also fine in your own way. Now you're working in Bangalore. Well, when did you leave Delhi and go to Bangalore?"

"Two months after our separation. Later when I was searching for you, I met with an accident. After my accident it took nearly 6 months to recover."

"Accident!! What accident happened? When did it happen? How did it happen? Tell me everything, Rishav."

"Yes. Of course. I'll tell you everything."

"Yes Rishav, I want to know. Why did such a big storm happen in our life? I will never forgive Sunil, but how did he do all these"

"Don't worry, Jiya. Sunil is not roaming free now. He is locked up."

"Really?"

"Yes, Jiya."

"Just tell me one thing, Rishav, how could you find me? I left our own country, I no longer use my social media account, and I created this profile on a social dating site with a fake name."

"Wait, Darling, wait for a while. I'll tell you everything."

Now Rishav continued to tell what happened one after another :

"When you left the house with your mother.. sorry, it was my mistake, I said so, I became very sad. I was missing you. I felt completely alone. After you left home, I gave some money to our maid and asked her to go back to her house. That night I also left our dream house as my dream was no longer with me then. That night my parents were very surprised to see me. Back home I was completely silent. I didn't talk to anyone for two days. Then I told everything at home. That day my sister Rohini came. So it was convenient to open my mind and tell everything to them. My mother loved Sunil very much. She was very hurt when she heard that you were going to him. Rohini didn't want to believe any of these. Then I showed everyone the proof sent by Sunil where you signed and gave everything to Sunil. I didn't want to stay in Delhi anymore. Always remembered you, missed you a lot, but could not see you. Just two months after we broke up I left with the posting at Bangalore. My mother died exactly a year and a half after I moved there."

Then I asked, "What are you saying, Rishav? Mom is no longer alive? And I know nothing of these."

Again Rishav continues, "How can you know, Jiya? You left India with our son and your mother and moved to New Jersey just a month before my mother died, without letting us know anything. You didn't try to contact me once after you left."

"Why would I contact you, Rishav? You drove me away without listening to my single word. That day you distrusted me, insulted my love. After I returned home, my parents wanted to talk to you and your family many times, to fix everything, but I requested them not to do this. I told my parents that if they talk to you or any of your family I will leave their house. I told my parents to trust their daughter and not to talk to that person who insulted their daughter. I told them to rely on me, and one day they will definitely be proud of their daughter."

"I know, Jiya, the mistake was on my part. My mother and Sunil told me many things before. But I never believed in anything. I just trusted you. So I never asked you anything about this before. But after seeing the proof sent by Sunil that day, I was very disappointed. That was the first time I misunderstood you, distrusted you. Even Rohini got confused to see that."

While talking, our coffee and food arrived on the table.

Rishav continued talking again, "I was not staying in Delhi after our separation. After my mother passed away, my father became all alone in our house in Delhi. Dad repeatedly requested me not to go back to Bangalore. I could not understand what to do then. Then

Rohini and Manish told me that they will take responsibility for our father, so I should not worry. It was decided that our father would stay with Rohini, and dad agreed with it. But then our two houses in Delhi would remain empty, one is our paternal house and another one is our dream house. So I thought I would sell our dream house before going back to Bangalore. So I went to arrange everything to remove all our belongings from that house. And what I found there changed all my decisions in an instant. When I left that house after you left, I didn't bring too many things with me, not even notice anything. But that day when I went to take our stuff from the house I noticed a medical file in our living room. Yours. I was very surprised to see the file. What happened to you, you didn't tell me anything. It was your pregnancy test report, you were pregnant for two months. I immediately went to your doctor with that report, from there to your rented flat in Delhi. I ran around looking for you all day. I was very disappointed not to find you anywhere. Then when I came to know from your neighbor that you moved to Chandigarh house at 6 months pregnant, I immediately left with my car to meet you. I took no one's word that day, did not even take anyone with me. I was driving thinking about you, my late mom and our baby. I was wondering how the baby looks, does it have beautiful eyes like yours? How is the baby's little face? I didn't notice when a truck came in front of me while driving too fast. To avoid it, I hit the road divider very hard. After that I can't remember anything. The accident happened that night on the Delhi Chandigarh Connecting National Highway. When I regained my consciousness, I felt unbearable pain all over my body and could not move. I was hospitalized for three months after that terrible accident. Then for another three months I stayed in Manish and Rohini's new house at Karol Bagh in Delhi. Then our father already started staying at their new house. That time was pathetic for me. Missed you all the time. You had already left the country, your phone number had changed, and I didn't know anything about this. After recovery I was looking for Sunil. But I did not know where their village house is in Odisha. Dad just couldn't remember properly. Maybe my mother knew, but she passed away. Sunil may have changed his phone number so that no one of us could contact him. Unable to do anything, I finally went back to Bengalore in desperation, seven months after my mother's death."

"Then how did you catch Sunil?"

"That's what I'm saying now, Jiya. After five months, again I had to go to Delhi From Bangalore on my mother's first death anniversary. It took place at our ancestral home in Kalkaji, Delhi. I returned to Bangalore after spending two days there. One month later, suddenly Rohini called me and told me to come to their Delhi's Karol Bagh house as soon as possible. Before I said anything, she said again that it is very urgent, I must have to come and she cannot be asked any questions about this. Sometimes Rohini does that, I do not understand anything. But I love and respect her very much. I could not discord with her words. The day after I arrived at their home, Rohini and Manish took me to Jatin's house. Jatin is the neighbour of their new house at Karol Bagh, and Manish's friend. Jatin is a lawyer, Sunil used to go to him about the legal matters of your business."

Now I interrupted Rishav and said, "Yeah right. After joining my mercantile firm, Sunil used to handle the legal side of the business. He introduced me to Jatin one day. Then Sunil repeatedly requested me to consult lawyer Jatin instead of our old lawyer. Since Sunil had previously managed his father's business, he had experience, so I accepted his request."

Rishav said, "That was Sunil's trick, the lawyer will be in contact with Sunil more than you. And Sunil knowingly suggested that you sign the papers before going home at night, he didn't show you all the signed papers the next day. More morning meetings were held, so that you get less time to scrutinize the signed documents, and before the end of the meeting, Sunil would go to the lawyer with all the files. You've signed a lot of papers that you've never had a chance to verify. You met with many clients who are not genuine, Sunil did this just to keep you busy all the time. Sunil had two advantages in this, you don't get time to check all the papers, and you return home too late. Another thing Sunil did with it, sometimes called me saying that, you love spending time with Sunil, so you don't want to come home early from your office."

"Rishav, you never told me this."

"Jiya, my dear, I never believed a single word of Sunil. But I don't know why, sometimes I used to get jealous when he said your name. Only the evidence he sent that day made me a total fool. And you know how Sunil did it?"

"I really want to know, Rishav, when did I transfer my everything to Sunil."

"Well, listen. All this we got to know from Jatin. With the help of Jatin, Sunil first started transferring everything to his own name little by little. He thought he would take over all your business and make you his own. But when we planned to go to Goa, he thought it would increase our closeness again. At first he merged his father's old business with your new business without informing you. The day we went to Goa, all bank accounts related to your business, everything else, even your office building you signed and gave it to him. And that day Sunil deliberately reached the airport very late, so that you don't get a chance to check any documents. Only one thing remained to be taken from you, the original deed of your office building. When you returned from Goa, Sunil went to his village with everything. He never got the chance to take the deed of the office building from you. Sunil didn't gain anything by embezzling everything from you. Sunil continued to make losses in business again very soon after you left. And started selling all your business assets one by one. After that, only your office building was left. And to discuss it, Sunil went to Jatin's house one day. That day Rohini was shocked to see him. And later Rohini and Manish went to Jatin's house to get news about you. When they came to know that you did not go to Sunil, they were very relieved. Then they called me. And then we decided that to find you, we have to catch Sunil. Jatin and Rohini's intelligence helped us catch Sunil. They planned how to catch him. First, Jatin called Sunil and told him to come to Jatin's house. Then knowingly Jatin told him that the original Deed can be in Jiya's house. And when Sunil left Jatin's house, two men continued to follow him for the next several days. My friend Police Inspector Gaurav helped me a lot in this regard. Those two men followed Sunil all day and night. And we replaced the original Deed with a copy and kept it at our home. Sunil kept an eye on our house for almost a month. Twice in every week he came to check everything outside our house, then one day he brought a man to check the locks. Sunil prepared well and then one night came to our house to steal that Deed. The two men who were following Sunil sent us messages just in time. We were carefully waiting for Sunil outside our house. Sunil also stole your jewellery. Sunil was caught red handed in front of our house with Deed's copy and jewellery box. I was very disappointed when we didn't get any news of you from Sunil. However, Sunil told us something that helped us to find you. He advised us to contact your friend Arushi."

"You mean Arushi already knew everything, Rishav? I am very angry with Aarushi, she never told me anything. And as you came to know from Arushi that I left the country and moved here, then why were you asking me so much on that dating site?"

"O my Jiya, please listen to me. I repeatedly requested Arushi not to tell you anything. But the first day when I tried to speak with Arushi, she hung up the phone angrily without talking to me. Then immediately my father called Arushi again. Then Arushi had a lot of talk with my father and Rohini. We searched and found your friend Arushi on social media, then Rohini gradually became her friend there. Later she shared her contact number with Rohini. Arushi helped me contact you on my father and Rohini's request. I got to know about you and Ronit from her. When Ronit was just four months old, you went out looking for a job. One day you suddenly met Arushi and after that she and her husband helped you get a job here. Then when Ronit was just one year old, you moved here with your family. Arushi used to send me your photos regularly. I got my son's photo from her. And meanwhile she kept convincing you to open an account on a social dating site. You opened an account and told Arushi everything. And then one day I messaged you there."

"You also created that account with a fake name, Rishav. And you only wrote 'hi' that day. Nothing more."

"A journey of a thousand miles also begins with a single step, Darling. I started with a very small step, because I had a long way to go. How long I have waited for this day. When you used to tell me how your days are going, Ronit's every little thing, I used to imagine those pictures in my mind. And I was eagerly waiting to see all of you. After waiting for so long, finally the day has arrived. At last we got to meet on this exciting coffee date."

"Thank you for this memorable coffee date. I'll keep this unforgettable moment in my heart forever. Now it's time to say bye, Rishav. Maybe we will meet somewhere again."

"Jiya, won't you...."

"I never accused you. I know it was just a situation that went against us. I've forgiven you long ago. But no, Rishav. I can never go back into your life anymore."

"I know. I am not requesting you to come back into my life. Instead, let me back into your life again. Please accept me, Jiya."

I placed my hands on Rishav's hands. We have never experienced such a beautiful sunset before. This sunset came into our lives with the promise of a new beautiful sunrise tomorrow.

www.ingramcontent.com/pod-product-compliance
Lightning Source LLC
LaVergne TN
LVHW061558070526
838199LV00077B/7100